CAROL CARRICK

Upside-Down Cake

illustrated by **Paddy Bouma**

Clarion Books · New York

Clarion Books
a Houghton Mifflin Company imprint
215 Park Avenue South, New York, NY 10003

The type for this book was set in 16/21-point Weiss.
The illustrations were executed in pencil.

Printed in the USA.

Library of Congress Cataloging-in-Publication Data
Carrick, Carol.
Upside-down cake / Carol Carrick ; illustrated by Paddy Bouma.
p.   cm.
Summary: A nine-year-old boy tries to come to terms with his grief and anger when his father
develops cancer, gradually becomes weaker and weaker, and then dies.
ISBN 0-395-84151-8
[1. Death—Fiction. 2. Grief—Fiction. 3. Cancer—Fiction. 4. Fathers and sons—Fiction.]
I. Bouma, Paddy, ill. II. Title.
PZ7.C2344Up   1999
[Fic]—dc21   98-52506
CIP
AC

KPT   10   9   8   7   6   5   4   3   2   1

For my sons, Christopher and Paul,
and for my brother, Andrew

I wish I could talk about Dad, at least with my friends. But I can see that it makes them uncomfortable. When I remember happy things, my good feelings bubble over, but when I think of something sad, it's like water building up behind a dam. Sometimes the sadness leaks out a little at a time, but I'm afraid if I keep holding it back it will rise until the dam bursts.

And that's why I'm telling you this story.

Chapter One

Last year Dad was forty on his birthday and I was nine on mine. We always celebrated on my birthday because it was the day before his. But we took turns picking out the cake. Last year Dad asked Mom to bake his favorite—pineapple upside-down.

The afternoon seemed to go awfully slow. My little sister, Katie, was taking her nap, and Dad and I were just sitting around, smelling that good cake smell from the kitchen and wishing dinner was over so we could eat dessert.

When the cake was done, I watched Mom turn it upside down on the plate. The pineapple slices made perfect rings in the topping of nuts and brown sugar.

Mom let me eat all the delicious gooey stuff left in the pan, but it only made me want more.

"Hey, Mom," I begged. "Do we have to wait? Couldn't we have just a teensy-weensy piece now? Just a taste?"

Mom said okay, so Dad squirted the whole can of whipped cream over the top till it sputtered. Then he got a fork for each of us and said, "Dig in!" I looked at him in amazement, but he stuck his fork right in the cake and took a big mouthful.

"Mmmmmm," he said.

I couldn't believe we were getting away with this.

I took a forkful, too. It was so good—I still remember how it tasted. Soon we were competing to see who could eat the most.

"Hey!" Mom said. "Save room for dinner!"

But Dad said, "Today's our birthday. We'll eat dinner tomorrow." He had whipped cream on his mustache. He even had some in his eyebrows.

I thought Mom would be mad, but instead she started laughing. And you know what she did then? She grabbed a fork for herself. I think she got ahead of us because Dad and I were laughing so hard we almost choked. I

remember our laughter because it was probably the last time we all had fun together.

For weeks after that Dad kept promising we'd play the computer game he'd given me. But when I reminded him, he'd say, "We'll do it later." Finally I got angry with him and stomped off. Now I feel bad about that.

"Play with your friends," Mom said.

"Everyone's busy," I told her. "Besides . . . it's Dad's day off. We were going to do something, just the two of us. He's always breaking his promises. I hate that!"

Mom sighed. "Your dad is tired."

"He's always tired," I complained. "Grouchy, too."

Mom looked through the doorway to see if Dad was still reading his paper. "He's not feeling well these days," she said softly, so he wouldn't hear.

"What's wrong with him?" I asked. "He looks fine to me."

"We're not sure," Mom said. "He's going to the hospital on Monday so the doctors can give him a thorough checkup."

"Monday!" Then he can't come to my soccer game, I thought, but I told myself that wasn't so important.

The doctors ran a lot of tests. A few days later Mom and Dad got the results. All Mom told me was that the doctors decided Dad needed an operation. "But you don't need to worry," she said.

Good, I thought. Whatever is wrong, the doctors will fix it. And then Dad'll be okay.

After the operation Mom and I went to see him. We got a sitter for Katie because she was too young to know how to act in a hospital. I felt a little nervous, but the visit went fine even though Dad looked kind of pale. A plastic bag was hanging on a pole near his bed. Something dripped from it through a tube attached to his arm, but he said it didn't hurt at all. I

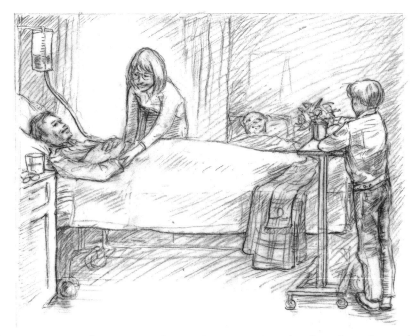

felt more at home when I saw Dad's bathrobe on the bed and his nail clippers and glasses on the bedside table. He was even wearing the pajamas we gave him for Father's Day.

The man in the bed next to Dad was really nice. He had a box of chocolates, and he said I could eat as many as I wanted.

Mom went to see Dad every night. I had to stay home with Katie, who is only four. I was supposed to make sure she ate all her dinner, which she never wanted to do. Once I got so mad at her that I ate her dessert, and she said she was going to tell Dad when he got home. I said she'd better not.

Two weeks later Mom went in the car after breakfast to bring Dad home. Katie and I waited for him the whole morning. We ran outside the minute the car pulled into the driveway. Dad took forever getting out, the way Grandma does when her knees are hurting. Katie was shy and put her fingers in her mouth, but I couldn't wait to throw myself on him.

I gave him a big hug, but he held me back a little.

"Hey, watch it, sport"—that's what Dad always called

me—"I'm a little sore, you know." It didn't sound like his voice.

"Oh, gosh," I said. "I'm sorry." He did look kind of shaky.

Still, I was disappointed. I thought he'd be happy to be home, but he didn't sound very happy. I wanted to tell him about my soccer games that he'd missed, and I thought we would do one of my puzzles or play checkers, maybe. Instead he said, "I'm going to lie down for a while." He seemed more like a guest than my dad.

Chapter Two

I expected everything to be the way it was before. After a few weeks Dad did go back to work at the real estate office, but when I got home from school, he'd be there already, sitting in his chair. The newspaper would be lying on his lap, but he wouldn't be reading it. "How's it going, sport?" he'd ask me in his new, tired-sounding voice.

"Okay," I'd say. And I would tell him about the B I got on my math test or how I'd sunk the most baskets that day in gym, but I could see he wasn't listening.

Pretty soon he was home all the time. "Isn't Dad going to work?" I asked after breakfast one Saturday. That used to be his busiest day, the day he sold the most houses to people.

Mom said she wanted to talk to me in my room. All the way upstairs I was thinking, This is not going to be good.

We sat opposite each other on my bed. "Dad is very sick," Mom said, rubbing my leg. "He's . . ." She started picking at a spot on my jeans, as if she was thinking about how to say the next words. I was holding my breath.

Tell me, I wanted to say.

"He has cancer."

Cancer. I wasn't exactly sure what that meant, but I definitely knew it was bad. I remembered when Grandpa had cancer. He was sick a long time.

"I'm sorry, honey." Mom scrunched up her shoulders in a discouraged sort of way. "The doctors did the best they could. But they can't really help him."

"Grandpa had cancer, and he got better." I made my voice sound hopeful. I still wanted to believe that Dad would be okay.

Mom was silent. Then she spoke so softly I could hardly hear her. "Dad isn't going to get better."

There was a buzzing noise in my head. My face was burning. How could this happen to my dad? He never got sick. He wasn't even that old.

"Mom . . . ?" I wanted to ask her if Dad was going to die. But she shook her head as if she couldn't answer. Her face was all crooked and smeary with tears. She patted my leg and then she got up and hurried out of the room.

I just sat there on my bed and stared out the window. I didn't want to go downstairs. Dad would be there. What could I say to him? I was scared.

As always, cars were going by in the street. I could see

Katie drawing on the sidewalk with chalk. She always drew the same thing—a cat made of circles with triangles for ears. Mr. Kelly across the street was raking leaves. It was crazy—how could people do ordinary stuff when something so bad was happening to us? My father was going to die.

There was a quiet knock on my door, and Dad came in. "Hey, sport, aren't you coming down?" He looked worn out—almost as though he was fading, except for

the bright red sweater he had on. I didn't want him looking like that. I wanted him to look strong.

My eyes squeezed shut. I beat my heels against the foot of the bed. It wasn't fair. I didn't want to lose Dad. Why was this happening? Nothing like this ever happened to any of the kids I knew.

Dad was holding me and I was crying. I pushed my face hard against his sweater—I can still feel the scratchy yarn against my skin. Dad started to say something, but then he sighed and hugged me tighter. I could hear him swallow.

Chapter Three

From then on, Dad spent more and more time in bed. When he was up, he just watched TV with Moby, our cat, on his lap. That was kind of funny—Dad didn't even like cats. And Moby never sat with anyone except Mom. He's mostly Mom's cat.

Dad was getting thin even though Mom cooked all his favorite foods, like meatloaf and mashed potatoes with lots of butter. He said they didn't taste right. At dinner Dad just sat there while we ate. He'd pick up his fork and put it down again. "Sorry, I'm not hungry," he'd say. Katie kept telling him he had to eat his vegetables. I told her to stop being a brat, but Dad held up his hand and said it was okay.

Still, I kept hoping that somehow he was going to get better. That the phone would ring and the doctor would tell Mom it was all a mistake—they had mixed up Dad with another patient. "Oh, thank goodness!" she would say, pressing her hand against her chest. Then she would look at us with a big smile on her face. And we would know. But that didn't happen.

I was afraid we wouldn't even have Christmas. I know that sounds pretty selfish. I thought Mom would be mad at me when I asked her about it. Instead, she kissed the top of my head and said, "Of course we will!"

I think Mom had to pick out all the presents herself. I helped her put Katie's dollhouse together. That was something Dad would have done, but by the time Katie was in bed, Dad was asleep, too. I couldn't wait to see the look on Katie's face when she saw the dollhouse on Christmas morning.

On Christmas Eve Mom asked me and Katie to decorate the tree—it would be a good surprise for Dad. I put on all the lights and ornaments. Well, most of them. Katie put some on, too, but she wasn't much help. You're supposed to put the big balls on the lower branches, but Katie put them on any old way and some got broken.

All the time we were decorating the tree, she was doing this little dance and singing me songs she had

learned in nursery school. I would never tell Katie this, but actually she made decorating the tree fun—she was so excited. She didn't understand about Dad yet.

When the tree was finished, Katie couldn't wait for Dad to see it, so she went upstairs and made him come down.

"Wow!" he said. He really looked surprised. "Did you do this all by yourselves?" he asked. And he laughed when Katie pulled him around the tree and showed him every ornament she had put on it.

"Great job! This is the best tree we've ever had," he kept saying.

I was glad because it was the first time he'd seemed happy about Christmas this year.

Everyone tried to make sure the holiday was a really good one. Grandma and Grandpa came to our house so we wouldn't have to drive all the way to theirs the way we usually did. Dad stayed downstairs the whole time. But he fell asleep in his chair after the big dinner Mom made, just the way Grandpa always does, even though it was only the middle of the day. His hair was getting thin like Grandpa's, too, and his sweater looked baggy on him.

While Grandma helped Mom with the dishes, I played with Katie and her dollhouse. It was the kind lots of little kids have, with plastic furniture and round wooden people. The whole family had smiley faces, even the dog. Katie made them hop around like they were walking, and she talked for them in a squeaky voice. She said the daddy was sick and had to stay in bed. She was the mother. I had to be the kids and the dog while she bossed us around.

Before it got dark I wanted to try out my new dirt bike, but Mom told me to wait so I could say good-bye to Grandma and Grandpa, who had to go home soon. Grandma gave me an extra squeeze when they left. I felt sad for them even though they tried to act cheerful, with smiley faces like Katie's doll people. Dad was their son and they could see how sick he was.

What would it be like if Dad wasn't here next Christmas? I didn't want to think about that. Instead I thought about my new dirt bike. Tomorrow I could try it out.

Chapter Four

Soon Dad left the house only when Mom drove him to see the doctor. Most of the time he slept, so we had to be quiet. Mom was always on the phone when I came home from school, talking to doctors or friends who called to see how Dad was. When I'd try to get her attention for a minute, just to tell her something, she'd wave me away.

We rented what Dad called "the steel monster," a hospital bed, and moved him into the family room next to the kitchen. The bed had railings we could pull up on the sides like a crib so Dad wouldn't fall out, and it took up most of the room. There was a button Dad could press to raise the head and foot of the bed when he wanted to sit up or put his feet up. The motor made a noise. Moby was so scared of it that he wouldn't come into the family room.

Katie seemed to think the bed was just another toy. She wanted to ride up and down on it, but Dad shook his head no. He wasn't feeling too good, he said.

For once Katie didn't whine, but she asked why Dad didn't sleep in his own bed. When I told her that he couldn't go up and down stairs anymore, she said, "Oh," and studied Dad seriously while she sucked on her thumb. She knew he was sick, but she kept forgetting it.

Dad kept the TV on all the time. After I did my homework in the kitchen, I got up on the bed with him and we would watch together. Sometimes after a really exciting part I'd turn to him and say, "Did you see that!" But he'd be sleeping. His cheeks were so bony now that he didn't look like my dad, and his mustache had gotten long and drooping. He needed a shave.

One evening in the middle of a show we were watching—it was about this dog who could ride a surfboard—Dad cleared his throat and asked me for a glass of water.

"Put it on the table," he said when I brought it. Instead of drinking it, he took hold of my hand. His eyes had dark circles around them, but they were still very blue. I was wondering what he wanted. "I love you, sport," he said, squeezing my hand. His voice was raspy. "I love you very much." He had never said that to me before.

"I love you, too," I mumbled, but I couldn't look at him. I was thinking, Why did he have to die? How could he let this happen? My hand lay in his without squeezing back. I kept staring at our hands so he wouldn't see how angry I was. His hand felt cold, and his fingernails looked clean and white next to mine.

"I have to go to bed," I said to get away from him. I feel awful now when I think about it—How could I have been so mean to him?

I worried about a lot of stuff: Would we have to sell our house and move away? What would Katie and I do if something happened to Mom, too? Live with Grandma and Grandpa?

Sometimes I lay in bed with my eyes shut and tried not to breathe. I wondered what it was like when someone died. I couldn't ask Mom. She might get upset.

Mom used to work at the library, but she was staying

home to take care of Dad now. When I made even a little mistake, like forgetting to feed Moby, she would lose her temper.

"You have to help," she'd say. "I can't do everything."

"I am, Mom. I'm trying."

How was I supposed to know what she wanted all the time? Pretty soon I was afraid to ask her to drive me to basketball practice or help me with my homework.

I stopped bringing friends home from school. We would have to be quiet, anyway, and it didn't seem right

to be having fun when Dad was so sick. I spent most of the time at my best friend Steve's house. Actually I was glad to be somewhere else. Sometimes, when we were shooting baskets, I forgot about Dad completely. Then I felt guilty.

Dad didn't have the strength to get out of bed anymore. He stopped eating—his arms were as thin as my wrist—and he couldn't even swallow the pills that he took for pain. The nurse who sometimes came to the house showed Mom how to give him his medicine in drops.

Mom and Katie and I went on having our meals, as always, in the room where he was. We talked in our normal voices and we didn't turn down the sound on the television when he was sleeping. Dad didn't seem to notice. Finally he stopped speaking altogether, and I wasn't sure he understood us when we talked to him.

Chapter Five

One night Dad had trouble breathing. Next morning when I opened my eyes, I felt something had happened. For one thing, I knew I had missed school because the sun was so bright.

Mom was standing in front of my window, turning the pages of her address book.

"Mom? What's the matter?" I asked.

She took my hand and sat down next to me on the bed. "Honey, Dad died early this morning. In his sleep."

I knew this day had to come—sometimes I had even wanted to get it over with. But still it was hard to believe.

Mom was stroking my hand. "He looks peaceful now. Would you like to see him?"

I didn't know.

Mom told me to get dressed while she woke up Katie. I was afraid of what it would feel like to see Dad. I had never seen a dead person. Katie was clutching her teddy bear. I sneaked a look at her as the three of us went downstairs, but she was watching each step as Mom led her down by the hand.

Dad lay with his hands folded on the blanket. His eyes were closed just as if he was sleeping. His face was very pale, but he looked younger somehow.

"You can tell him good-bye," Mom said gently.

I touched his pajama sleeve. "Good-bye, Dad," I whispered. Saying it, I got a really hard lump in my throat and I started to cry. Then Mom cried, too, and so did Katie. I think Katie was crying because we were—she wasn't used to seeing us like that. Mom kneeled down and hugged us and we cried together, but quietly, as though we didn't want to disturb Dad.

The phone rang. Mom asked me to fix Katie some cereal. I didn't want any because I had this ache in my stomach. Then she told us to go upstairs and watch TV in her room. Later, when we came down, Dad was gone. They'd taken him to the funeral home, Mom said. The hospital bed was gone, too.

From then on the house was full of voices and people. The phone rang and rang. Neighbors dropped off all kinds of food. Grandma and Grandpa came, and aunts and uncles and cousins that I hadn't seen for a long time. I was so excited to be with them all that for a second I forgot why they were there.

The relatives made a big fuss over Katie, so she showed off a lot. She brought out her dollhouse for them to see and even did her Christmas dance, holding her dress up so high that her underpants showed. The little boys rolled around on the floor and giggled. She laughed, too.

At bedtime Mom wanted me to read to Katie so she would calm down and go to sleep. Right in the middle of the story, Katie asked me, "When is Dad coming back?"

"I told you before," I said. "Dad is in heaven. He's not coming back."

Katie pouted.

When Mom came to say good night, I asked her, "Do you think Dad can see us and hear us?"

Mom shook her head. "I don't really know," she said. "Nobody does. I just know he's alive in our memories of him—he's alive to me."

Downstairs, people were still talking. There was so much going on that I only got to thinking about Dad when I was by myself in bed. I didn't want to picture him lying in the funeral home. Was he cold and alone there? I wished I had spent more time with him while he was sick, and I wished I had done more to make him happy.

Chapter Six

I had never been to a funeral. I wasn't sure I wanted to go.

Mom said, "Don't worry. You'll sit next to me and hold my hand. It'll just be our friends and family there—to say good-bye to Dad."

Katie stayed home with my little cousins. At the time I thought she was lucky, but now I'm glad I went. I sat next to Mom in the front row with Grandma and Grandpa and my uncles and aunts.

I didn't want to listen when the minister started saying good things about Dad. I didn't want to think about Dad at all—because I was not going to cry in front of all those people. Instead I jiggled my foot until Mom put her hand on my leg to stop me. Then I squinted at the candles until the flames grew into stars, and after that I counted the panes in the stained-glass window.

Everything was fine until we sang a hymn I had learned in Sunday school. It's one I like a lot, only my voice cracked when I started to sing. Tears began running down my face and making big wet spots on my shirt. I wiped my face very carefully with one finger so no one would notice. Grandpa's arm went around my shoulder, and when I peeked up at him, his cheeks were wet, too. So it was okay to cry.

When the service was over, Mom and I, Grandpa and Grandma, and the rest of the family had to walk up the aisle to the door of the church so we could say "Thank you for coming" to people as they left. Some of them were our neighbors and the people who worked in Dad's office, but some of them I'd never seen before. It made me feel good—and bad, too—to hear everyone say how much they had cared about Dad.

I was surprised to see that Steve and his mother had come. His mom hardly even knew my dad. She patted me on the shoulder and said, "Steve and I miss you. Come see us soon."

Steve looked uncomfortable and serious in his dress-up clothes. I wished I could could go home with him right then and shoot baskets or something.

When I woke up the next morning, the house was quiet. I couldn't believe that Dad was gone. I hoped maybe this was some kind of bad dream and Dad would be downstairs having breakfast. But of course he wasn't.

I stayed out of school the rest of the week. It was strange to be home when I wasn't even sick. During the day I would think: My class is eating lunch without me, or: They're out on the playground now.

The kids in my class sent me a big card to say how sorry they were, and they all signed their names on it. It made me feel special.

When I went back to school, teachers came up to me in the hall to say hello. Even the principal put his arm around my shoulder. I wished they would stop—it was embarrassing.

The kids acted nice, too—I was one of the first to be chosen when we picked kickball teams at recess. None of them said anything about Dad, though. I guess it made them feel funny.

Steve and I were in the cafeteria a couple days after I went back. Markie—we usually call him Wood Tick because he's so small—was telling us his dad had caught a twenty-pound striped bass.

"My dad caught a twenty-five-pounder last spring," I said. "I was with him." I spoke loud because the room was so noisy.

Suddenly everyone at our end of the table went quiet. Steve picked up his tray. "C'mon," he said. "Let's go outside."

I guess I wasn't supposed to talk about my dad. I didn't even say his name much around Mom, because I thought it might make her feel bad.

It was hard being in school, pretending to pay attention in class and acting as though I was okay. Soon the kids were treating me as if things were back to normal again. At least for them.

Chapter Seven

School is out for the summer now, and you know what's really scary? When I can't even remember Dad's face or what his voice was like. But then, just when I think I'm getting used to him being gone, some little thing will happen, like seeing his sweater in the closet, and it starts me crying again.

Sometimes Mom wears his sweater, so it doesn't smell like him anymore. And when she hugs me they're nice hugs, but not like hugs from him. When Dad gave me one of his bear hugs, I couldn't breathe. I used to yell, "Cut it OUT!"—but it made me feel safe.

I was eating corn flakes, my usual afternoon snack,

when Mom came home from work at the library. She was carrying two supermarket bags.

Now that I was supposed to help more around the house, I asked, "Any more stuff to carry in?"

"Nope. Thank you." She set the bags on the counter and started putting the groceries away.

"Here," she said, passing me a carton of ice cream. "Put this in the freezer, will you?"

Then she asked, "How about a party this year?"

I made a face. My tenth birthday was just a week away, and I'd been thinking about it. With Dad gone, it was going to be the worst birthday I ever had.

"Parties are for kids," I said, turning my back. I didn't want to talk to her about it.

"You're a kid, aren't you?" she asked, messing up my hair.

I jerked my head away. "I just don't feel like having one."

"Then what kind of birthday cake shall I make?"

I shrugged. "I don't care," I mumbled. "Look . . . I'm sorry, Mom. I'm in a bad mood."

"Fine," she said, but she was not about to give up. "The party won't be till next week, when it's your birthday, and you'll be in a better mood."

I took a huge breath and puffed it out. "How am I supposed to be happy and have a party when . . ." I didn't want to say it and make her feel bad.

"When your father has died?"

I didn't expect her to say that. Instead of answering, I put my bowl in the sink and rinsed it out.

"Sweetie, your dad would want you to have fun."

"How am I going to have fun?" I asked, raising my voice. "The kids all treat me like a freak!"

"Oh, honey." She hugged me. "That's not true. Is it?"

She tried to take my hands, but I pulled away from her. "Not really," I admitted. But I knew they'd feel weird coming over here, even for a party.

"Maybe they don't know what to say," she offered.

"They're afraid I'll go and cry on them."

Katie heard Mom's voice and came running in with one of her stupid dolls. "Her hair came off! Fix it. Fix it," she begged, tugging on Mom's sweatshirt. Katie always butts in like that.

"I'm telling Mom something," I yelled at her. "Will you shut up!"

Mom ignored me and touched Katie's cheek. "Say 'Excuse me,' Katie," she said, and she looked through the junk drawer for some glue. Mom spoils Katie a lot more than she used to. She says Katie needs more attention now that Dad is gone.

That made me mad.

"Katie doesn't miss Dad at all," I said after she went outside with her doll stuff. "At least she doesn't act like it."

"That's because she's so little." Mom tilted her head and looked at me as though I was a little kid, too. "She doesn't understand what's happened . . . not really. But

notice how she's sucking her thumb again, the way she did when she was a baby?"

"Okay," I said. "So I'm jealous." I said it as though I didn't mean it, but I did. "And I'm jealous of Steve, too. He couldn't play with me today 'cause he gets to do something with his father on Wednesdays."

Mom looked disappointed with me. "But Steve doesn't see his dad that much." Steve's parents are divorced.

"At least he *has* a father," I shouted. "I'm never going to see mine again." And I stamped out of the kitchen.

Mom came after me and grabbed me by my shoulders. She put her arms around me in the dark hallway and held me tight until I quit struggling to break free from her. At last I stopped holding my breath and let it out. It sounded more like a sob. Mom relaxed her grip.

"I got used to it when Dad was really sick," I said into her shoulder. "And I knew he was probably going to die. But I can't get used to him never coming back. I just can't! I need him sometimes. I want to tell him stuff."

"I know," she murmured. So I was surprised a moment later when she gave a little chuckle.

"What is it?" I said, lifting my head.

"Oh, I was just thinking about the time your friend

Peter was over. And he hit you in the head with a rock. Remember?"

I nodded.

"He did it 'cause I told him I couldn't get hurt."

"Dad and I heard you scream," Mom said, "and we ran out into the yard. When we saw your face all bloody, it scared us half to death. You were just a little kid then."

She smiled. "It turned out the cut wasn't so bad. You

were crying mostly because you were angry. You told Dad you were being Superman."

I laughed. "And I really thought the rock couldn't hurt me. That was pretty dumb."

"You said you were gypped. And Dad felt bad about it, even though it sounds funny now. He didn't want you to be hurt or disappointed about anything. He wanted to always be there for you—to protect you from feelings like that. But he couldn't. Nobody can, really."

Mom hugged me again and I put my head against her shoulder. We just stood there like that. And then she squeezed me. "Things will get better," she said. "Trust me."

Chapter Eight

That week I had my first dream about Dad. In my dream he was making breakfast as if he'd never been gone. The sun was pouring through the window behind him.

"Dad!" I said. "You're alive!" It was just him and me there in the kitchen.

He laughed. "How's it going, sport?" he said. His face was tan and smooth as if he had just come back from a wonderful vacation. And this big smile broke out under his mustache. When he smiled at me like that, I always felt I was the best.

I wished the dream would go on and on—I was so happy.

When I woke up, I still had that feeling.

"So, did you change your mind about the party?" Mom asked before I left for school.

"No," I said. But this time I didn't get angry.

"Your birthday's tomorrow," she reminded me, as if I didn't know. "What kind of cake should I make?"

I thought about the dream and how I wanted it to last.

"Pineapple upside-down cake," I said suddenly. "With lots of whipped cream. And three forks—just for you and Katie and me."

Mom smiled, and I could tell she was remembering last year.

"No—four forks," I said. "I think I'll invite Steve."

64